The Story of My Life

By Heather E. Schwartz

Illustrated by Linda Silvestri

Publishing Credits

Rachelle Cracchiolo, M.S.Ed., *Publisher*
Conni Medina, M.A.Ed., *Editor in Chief*
Nika Fabienke, Ed.D., *Content Director*
Véronique Bos, *Creative Director*
Shaun N. Bernadou, *Art Director*
Seth Rogers, *Editor*
Valerie Morales, *Associate Editor*
Kevin Pham, *Graphic Designer*

Image Credits

Illustrated by Linda Silvestri

Library of Congress Cataloging-in-Publication Data

Names: Schwartz, Heather E., author. | Silvestri, Linda, illustrator.
Title: The story of my life / by Heather E. Schwartz ; illustrated by Linda Silvestri.
Description: Huntington Beach, CA : Teacher Created Materials, [2020] | Includes book club questions. | Audience: Age 13. | Audience: Grades 4-6. | Summary: "Seventh grade isn't going so well for Lexi. Stuck in a remedial gym class -- and stumped for ideas for a playwriting contest she wants to enter -- she's convinced she'll never be able to reach her dreams. Then, to her surprise, she discovers she's been working toward them all along"-- Provided by publisher.
Identifiers: LCCN 2019031459 (print) | LCCN 2019031460 (ebook) | ISBN 9781644913567 (paperback) | ISBN 9781644914465 (ebook)
Subjects: LCSH: Readers (Elementary) | Physical education and training--Juvenile fiction. | Overweight children--Juvenile fiction. | Playwrighting--Juvenile fiction. | Middle schools--Juvenile fiction.
Classification: LCC PE1119 .S447 2020 (print) | LCC PE1119 (ebook) | DDC 428.6/2--dc23
LC record available at https://lccn.loc.gov/2019031459
LC ebook record available at https://lccn.loc.gov/2019031460

5301 Oceanus Drive
Huntington Beach, CA 92649-1030
www.tcmpub.com
ISBN 978-1-6449-1356-7
© 2020 Teacher Created Materials, Inc.

Table of Contents

CHAPTER ONE

Just Another Day in (Remedial) Gym Class

Did you know there's a thing called remedial gym class? Probably not. I never heard of it either until I found out I was in it when I got to middle school last year.

"Lexi's in remedial gym because

she's overweight," I heard Veronica whisper to Suzette, which is not true. Yes, I'm overweight and that's a fact, but hasn't she ever seen a YouTube video? Plenty of bigger people are good at yoga and gymnastics and all kinds of sports. I just don't happen to be one of them.

When math was over, the bell rang, and it was time for the class I dreaded most. I trailed behind Veronica and Suzette on their way to the gym. They're in regular PE, but the teachers put up a divider that cuts the gym in half. Ms. Kaminski teaches on one side and Ms. Becker on the other. The divider makes it so our classes can't see each other. I'm not sure if they do it to be nice so the other kids don't watch and make fun of us. It could also be because they don't want the athletic kids picking up any bad habits.

In the locker room, I took my gym clothes into a bathroom stall and changed really fast because it's the only way to get any privacy. Then, I hurried out to the gym. I may belong here, but I'll be honest: I'm not happy about it. One problem is I don't have any friends in this class. Last year, PE was actually fun with my best friend, Lucy, since she'd pick me for teams and help me cheat on my sit-ups. Another problem is it's completely embarrassing—and I'm starting to think I'm actually the worst one in here.

The class formed a clump on the floor while we waited for Ms. Becker. You can tell just by looking why some of us are here. Emma's knee is wrapped in a bandage. She has a sports-related injury and is just working her way back into the regular class. Other girls have hidden "athletic deficiencies," like me. It's definitely not all about size. Maha is also overweight, but Phoebe, for example, looks really fit but has no

coordination.

"All right! On your feet, ladies!"
Ms. Becker yelled, stepping through the
door in the divider.

We all got up from the floor
awkwardly, and in a few minutes, we
were practicing passing a basketball.
Sounds easy, right? Just throw and
catch. Well, a couple of minutes after
that, I was headed down to the nurse
with a bloody nose, so you can see who

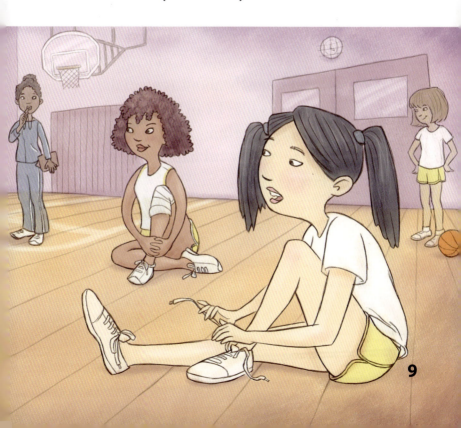

9

hasn't mastered catching.

In the nurse's office, I had to wait my turn behind a whole line of kids. I held my nose in a wad of tissues and stared at a poster on the wall. "Could you be the author of our next school play?" the poster asked in crooked magic-marker letters. "Enter today!"

I couldn't think of a single topic to write about with my nose pounding to the beat of my heart. But the idea of entering the contest was still exciting. I love writing for school, and I've kept a diary since third grade. Unfortunately, this year it's mostly about remedial gym. It seems like I can't go a single day without something really weird or embarrassing or awful happening in that class.

Dear Diary

November 2

Note: Names have been changed to protect the humiliated.

Mona and I started talking in gym today while I was fake counting sit-ups for her. She said she's going to New York City to see a play, and she's really excited because she wants to be an actress—and also her aunt **wrote** the play! Now, I'm inspired to write the rest of this entry in play form.

Scene: Goodwin Middle School gym. Everyone is looking at Ms. Bitner, except Lani, who's dramatically staring off into space with her mouth hanging open because she can't get enough oxygen in through her nose ever since it got bashed in with the basketball.

Ms. Bitner: Great news! You're ready to move into the regular class today! (She rushes away.)
Lani looks around frantically, and when Emily catches her eye, looking happy, Lani assumes she should go with her to the other side of the gym.

Random Kids: Yay! You're back! (This is said only to Emily. Lani feels dumb.)

Ms. Kowalski: OK, girls, let's make sure you're in the game first!
Lani pretends to tie her sneaker, which actually has a hook and loop strap.

Ms. Kowalski: Come on, Lani! Be aggressive!

The game starts, and a teammate tries to pass Lani the ball, but it bounces right through her legs. Suddenly, an earsplitting whistle startles Lani, and in an instant, she decides to prove herself. She races to grab the ball from the sidelines and tries to dribble it across the floor. When she's close to the basket, she shoots, but loses her balance and falls into Emily. Meanwhile, the ball hits a folding chair (knocking it over with a deafening crash) and bounces directly into Ms. Kowalski's face, sending her glasses flying.

Emily: My knee! My knee! (Emily is rolling around in pain.)

Ms. Kowalski: My glasses! My glasses! (Ms. Kowalski is on her hands and knees feeling around for her glasses.)

Random Teammate #1: You're supposed to stop when you hear the whistle.

Random Teammate #2: That wasn't even the right basket!

Ms. Bitner: (sticking her head through the door of the divider) Oh Lani, there you are! Did you forget you're supposed to be in our special class?

Spotlight on Lani. Everyone watches her walk across the gym back through the door to the remedial side. Ms. Bitner wasn't even talking to her about moving to the regular class. She only meant Emily—who may be back if Lani wrecked her knee all over again.

CHAPTER THREE

Think Positive!

I complain a lot about gym class, but school really isn't that bad. My mom says I should focus on the positive, which might be her way of saying I sound whiny. Just in case, I've decided to limit my complaints to my diary. In real life, I'll pretend the class doesn't exist.

"It's only 50 minutes—and not even every day. Just on school days," Lucy reminded me when I told her at lunch.

I was about to point out that most days are school days, but I stopped myself.

"Right…So, did you get a good grade on your social studies essay?" I asked, carefully steering the conversation away from this negativity.

Personally, I was ecstatic about my own grade. We had to write one page of historical fiction about American Indian life, and I included all sorts of details to get 10 out of 10 points on it. The teacher wrote a comment: "Your characters are very realistic!"

"Seven points," Lucy answered, as Maha headed over and set down her lunch tray. She's been eating with us lately, too. "What about you?"

I'd outscored her, but Lucy didn't mind.

"Hey, you should enter that contest for the school play," she said thoughtfully. "Imagine seeing kids act out a story you wrote!"

I sighed. "Actually, I've been trying to work on that, but the imagination part of my brain is on a permanent vacation." I swiveled to face Maha. "How does your aunt do it anyway?"

She shrugged and picked up her slice of pizza. "Did I tell you her play is selling out?"

"Oh, come on, you can write a play," Lucy cut in. "Write me a little part so I won't have too many lines to memorize."

"Yeah, you're a great writer. Look at your grades," Maha agreed, adding, "I'll take a major role, please."

I couldn't help thinking even stellar grades had nothing to do with being an awesome creative writer. There was no way I'd grow up to sell out theaters with my amazing abilities to write school essays. I could just picture the marquee at my first show: "Please describe the steps of the mummification process used in ancient Egypt."

Actually, the topic itself was pretty interesting—but it definitely didn't sound like a play!

After lunch, Maha and I went to the gym to practice shooting hoops during our free period. It's not helping, but we made it fun. We bounced the ball back and forth, and on each bounce, the

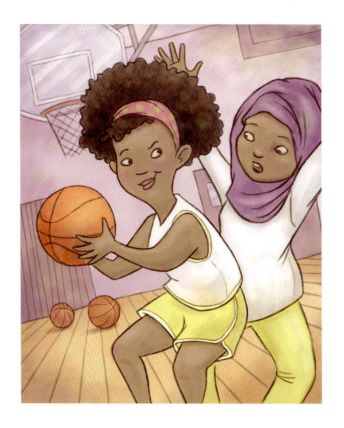

person who threw it yelled an idea for a play I could write.

"A girl can't convince her parents to buy her a phone, and then aliens bring her one," I suggested, bouncing the ball to Maha.

On her turn, Maha shouted, "A family of sloths adopts a human child."

I laughed. "Sure—maybe you should write that one."

That night, I still couldn't come up with an idea I really liked. Too bad I couldn't be in Remedial Imagination Class. Now that would be fun! I wrote about the idea in my diary. Then, I did my biology homework and wrote about my latest disaster in gym class, when I tipped over a basket of tennis balls. (See what I mean about my lack of improvement?)

By the time I finished, I was too exhausted to work on a play. I fell asleep with my biology papers, notebooks, and diary piled around me in bed.

CHAPTER FOUR

The Joke's on Me

In the morning, my alarm didn't go off, so when I woke up, I thought it was Saturday. The smell of pancakes drifted under my bedroom door. I climbed out of bed and headed to the kitchen, where everything started to go wrong.

"You're wearing pajamas!" my mother said when she saw me. "The bus will be here in five minutes!"

Ugh—it was Friday! I ran back to my bedroom and threw on some clothes, then scooped up all the papers off my bed and shoved them into my backpack. If there's one thing I hate, it's running for the bus while everyone on it watches and waits.

I made the bus only to learn my day would get even worse at school. First, my backpack ripped outside the cafeteria, and all my stuff fell out. Ballpoint pens and pencils rolled away while important papers slid across the floor. I dodged people's feet to grab everything, then lugged it all to my locker, where the combination took five tries before it would open. And then—surprise!—I was late to homeroom.

My first class was PE, and needless to say, I was not ecstatic. I was frustrated about my morning, and I had all this adrenaline coursing through my veins that made me jittery. We were working on running while dribbling the basketball, then trying to make a basket without stopping. I jogged across the gym, dribbling the ball in front of me. *You think I can't do this? I'll show you,* I thought, feeling the energy inside me pulse into my fingertips.

And would you believe I actually made it in—that time and four more times?

"Way to go, Lexi!" Ms. Becker cheered, while Maha and the other kids actually clapped.

I couldn't keep myself from blushing and smiling. Four baskets isn't just luck. I didn't think I was getting any better, but practicing with Maha must have really helped!

At lunch with Lucy and Maha, I was eager to discuss my victory, but the next table was being really noisy. We couldn't even hear each other, so we all turned to see what the commotion was about. Just then, Veronica and Suzette burst out laughing.

"Read some more!" urged another girl at their table.

"You're supposed to stop when you hear the whistle," Veronica read.

I had a weird sense of déjà vu, like I'd heard those words before. More kids were listening now.

"That wasn't even the right basket!" she continued. Everyone laughed again, and I suddenly realized those words were my own. Somehow, Veronica had my diary—I must have brought it to school by accident and dropped it when my backpack tore open!

I jumped up, grabbed it from her mid-sentence, and raced out of the cafeteria. Could anything be worse than hearing the story of your miserable life read out loud at school? Everyone was laughing, like I was a big joke!

This was worse than any humiliation I'd ever suffered in gym class. I was so embarrassed, I didn't even want to face Maha for our practice session. I went to study hall instead, where I was sure I heard kids whispering about me, and by the end of the period, I couldn't take it. I got a pass to the nurse and hid on a cot for the rest of the day, then went home to hide in my room. Forever.

CHAPTER FIVE

Surprise Ending

When Lucy's number appeared on caller ID later that evening, I answered because she was literally the only person on Earth I was willing to talk to on the phone.

"Your play is hilarious!" she exclaimed. "But how come you gave it to Veronica?"

"My play? I didn't write any play—that was my diary! She found it in the hall!"

"But it sounded like a play…"

"I was just trying something. That was my diary Veronica read out loud today. It's a nonfiction story!"

"Oh no, I'm so sorry!" Lucy said, falling silent for a few seconds. Then, she continued, "Seriously, though, it was so exaggerated and funny—everybody loved it!"

I grabbed my diary, noticing from the outside it looked like a regular notebook. I flipped through the pages and realized I never wrote the words "Dear Diary," just the date. But I was still upset and refused to give in.

"Well, I'm really glad my disaster of a life is such great entertainment," I grumbled sarcastically.

Lucy is my best friend for a reason. She wasn't about to back down either.

"Well, you should be glad," she said, firmly. "Because it is."

"Can you hang out this weekend?" Lucy asked.

"Sorry, I have to work on my play," I answered, suddenly realizing that was exactly what I needed to do.

It was so strange. I came home thinking what happened in the cafeteria was the worst thing imaginable. Now, I realized I'd written a scene funny enough to make kids laugh out loud. I

flipped through my diary, reading other entries I'd written about gym class. When I imagined they were about someone else, they really did sound funny. I could use all of this material to write a play about a gym-class loser who found a way to triumph in the end. So what if it happened to be about my own life? Nobody had to know that. And even if they figured it out, I wasn't sure I minded.

By the end of the weekend, I was finished. I practically floated to the main office to turn in my play. I wasn't even surprised a few weeks later when I got the news in a special announcement at our monthly assembly: I won!

The same day I won the playwriting contest, Ms. Becker surprised me with even more amazing news.

"Lexi, I'm putting you on an accelerated track to move on from our remedial class," she said. "While you're still with us, would you be Maha's in-class coach and work with her on her athletic skills?"

"Me?" I asked, automatically. I didn't want to make that mistake again!

Ms. Becker nodded, so I glanced over at Maha and immediately knew that look on her face. She felt like a failure, and for the first time all year, I wasn't so eager to put remedial gym class behind me.

"I'd love to," I said, giving Maha a big grin.

I was still in remedial gym, but everything was different now. In a flash, I imagined coaching my new friend so well she'd leave the class with me when I did. I saw her landing the lead in my winning play, and I pictured us both getting roses on opening night. My head was practically bursting with positive thoughts.

"You can do it," I said, meaning both of us and all my dreams. "I know you can!"

About Us

The Author
Heather E. Schwartz is a writer who lives in upstate New York with her husband, two sons, and two cats. She performs at The Mopco Improv Theatre, making up scenes and songs on the spot. She also enjoys downhill skiing. Growing up, she could have benefitted from remedial gym class.

The Illustrator
Linda Silvestri is an illustrator and graphic designer in Southern California. When not prying one of three cats from her drawing board, you can find her working out of the home she shares with her husband, Tom.